FLOWER FAIRIES of the WINTER

~ A ~

CELEBRATION

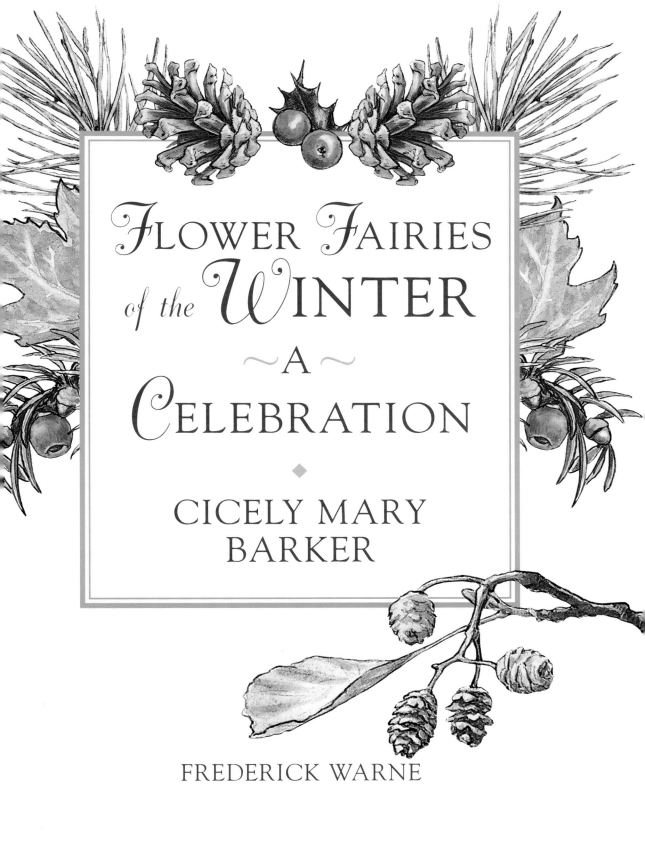

Flower Fairies of the Winter

~ A ~

Celebration

◆

CICELY MARY
BARKER

FREDERICK WARNE

The reproductions in this book have been made using the most modern electronic scanning methods from entirely new transparencies of Cicely Mary Barker's original watercolours. They enable Cicely Mary Barker's skill as an artist to be appreciated as never before.

FREDERICK WARNE

Published by the Penguin Group
27 Wrights Lane, London W8 5TZ, England
Penguin Putnam Inc., 375 Hudson Street, New York, New York 10014, USA
Penguin Books Australia Ltd, Ringwood, Victoria, Australia
Penguin Books Canada Ltd, 10 Alcorn Avenue, Toronto, Ontario, Canada M4V 3BN
Penguin Books (NZ) Ltd, Private Bag 102902, NSMC, Auckland, New Zealand
Penguin Books (South Africa) (Pty) Ltd, 5 Watkins Street, Denver Ext 4, Johannesburg 2094, South Africa

Penguin Books Ltd, Registered Offices: Harmondsworth, Middlesex, England

Flower Fairies of the Winter first published in 1985
This edition first published by Frederick Warne 2001
1 3 5 7 9 10 8 6 4 2

ISBN 0 7232 4745 5

Text by Anna Trenter
Illustrations on pages 11-15 reproduced by kind permission of Martin Barker and Geoffry Oswald
Colour reproduction by Saxon Photolitho Ltd, Norwich
Printed in China by Midas Printing Ltd

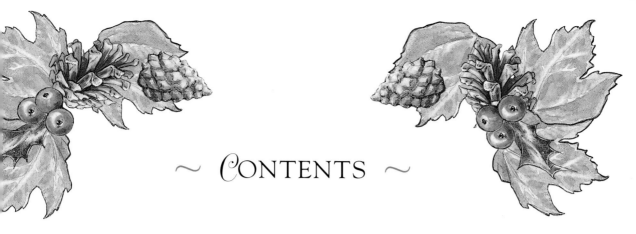

~ Contents ~

~ CONTENTS ~
(CONTINUED)

~ CICELY MARY BARKER ~

Above: A portrait of Cicely in her teens.

Below: Cicely (left) with her older sister Dorothy as children.

Cicely Mary Barker was born on 28 June 1895 in Croydon, South London. She was the second child of Mary and Walter Barker. Cicely was never very strong. She suffered from epilepsy and was sheltered from the outside world by her parents and her older sister, Dorothy. The Barkers were a comfortable middle class family. They employed a nanny to educate Cicely at home and a cook to prepare her special meals. They were also a close family, and despite her ill-health, Cicely enjoyed a happy childhood, making up for the lack of physical strength by an active imagination and a keen interest in drawing.

Cicely's talent was evident from an early age. Her father, a partner in a seed supply company, was a capable watercolourist and he nurtured her early aptitude. When the family went on holiday, Cicely and Walter would sketch together by the seaside. At only thirteen years old, Cicely was enrolled in a correspondence course in art tuition. That same year, 1908, she exhibited her work at the Croydon Art

Society. Three years later, Cicely's father sold four of her drawings to the printer Raphael Tuck. Cicely also won second prize in the Croydon Art Society poster design competition and was elected a life member of the society. Already she was on her way to a successful artistic career. Sadly, Walter Barker did not live to witness his daughter's rise to fame. He died in 1912 at the age of forty-three. Mary and her two daughters sought comfort in their strong Christian faith, but they were facing straitened economic circumstances. It was Dorothy, the more practical of the two sisters, who assumed the role of main breadwinner. Trained as a teacher, she began to teach a kindergarten class, and it was her salary that enabled Cicely to continue to pursue her artistic goals.

The first editions of Flower Fairies of the Spring *and* Summer, *1923.*

Cicely contributed to the household finances by selling her poems and artwork to magazines such as *Child's Own*, *My Magazine* and Raphael Tuck annuals. She also painted a series of watercolour postcards on patriotic themes, popular during the First World War, as well as producing a set of six *Fairy Cards*, a charming precursor of her later work.

It was between 1917 and 1918 that Cicely began the project that was to make her a household name. The Flower Fairies illustrations merged two of her favourite subjects – children and nature. Cicely loved to paint directly from nature, influenced in this by her favourite Pre-Raphaelite artists. She made numerous sketches of flowers to ensure that her drawings were botanically accurate. She filled at least one sketchbook a year for all of her working life, leaving behind a rich collection of botanical drawings. Cicely used local children as models and she was fortunate in having many willing young relatives to draw.

Cicely almost always sketched the plant from life before she incorporated it into a fairy painting, as with this study of a pine cone for the Pine Tree Fairy.

A pastel by Cicely of Storrington where she spent the last years of her life.

She skilfully conveyed the child's personality as well as the flower's appearance. When the pictures were complete Cicely wrote poems to accompany the illustrations.

In 1923 Cicely decided that the first Flower Fairies book, *Flower Fairies of the Spring,* was ready to find a publisher. After several rejections, Blackie accepted the work and paid her £25 for twenty-four poems and paintings. The book was very popular and Blackie soon realised that they had a commercial success on their hands. Cicely, however, was a very unworldly character, protected by her mother and sister from the outside world. It was Mary who ensured that Cicely received royalties for her work. Cicely's ignorance of business allowed her to retain the innocence and simplicity that are so evident in her pictures and rhymes.

Mary and her daughters moved to a smaller house in Croydon in 1924, where

Dorothy established her own kindergarten and Cicely built a studio in the garden. Dorothy's pupils were another wonderful source of models for the Flower Fairies, and Cicely went on to produce a total of seven books for Blackie. Today there are eight Flower Fairies titles in print. In 1985, Cicely's publishers compiled the volume *Flower Fairies of the Winter* from existing works, so there is now a book for every season.

The Flower Fairies were not Cicely's only work. She wrote and illustrated two classic tales of her own, *The Lord of the Rushie River* and *Groundsel and Necklaces*, as well as illustrating several collections of rhymes. Cicely and her sister were regular church-goers, and Cicely painted many religious pictures. A collaboration between the sisters produced a book of Bible stories, *He Leadeth Me*. Cicely also painted church panels and altar pieces, such as *The Parable of the Great Supper* which hangs in St. George's Church, Waddon.

In 1954 Dorothy died unexpectedly of a heart attack. Cicely took over responsibility for housekeeping and looking after her elderly mother. This left little time for painting and Cicely was unable to continue her commercial career. On her mother's death in 1960, Cicely moved from Croydon to Storrington in Sussex, where there was a thriving artists' colony and where she had spent many happy holidays.

On 16 February 1973 Cicely herself died at the age of seventy-seven. Her ashes were scattered in a glade in Storrington churchyard, where she could remain close to the Sussex countryside that she so loved. Her spirit still endures in her Flower Fairies, which delight new generations of children more than seventy-five years after they first appeared.

Cicely in 1963.

15

~ ABOUT ~
FLOWER FAIRIES OF THE WINTER

Cicely Mary Barker published seven collections of Flower Fairy paintings—for *Spring, Summer, Autumn,* the *Garden,* the *Wayside, Trees* and a *Flower Fairy Alphabet.* In 1985, twelve years after her death, her then publisher Blackie reissued the whole series and decided to change the arrangement. By extracting appropriate Flower Fairies from the seven existing books, they were able to compile a volume of *Flower Fairies of the Winter.* This new set of eight titles, which now included a Flower Fairies book for every season of the year, proved extremely popular and the books have continued to be published in this way ever since.

A large number of the Winter Flower Fairies originally appeared as Flower Fairies of the Autumn, but Snowdrop, Dead-Nettle, Shepherd's Purse, Groundsel and Hazel-Catkin were Spring fairies, Winter Jasmine and Winter Aconite were Garden fairies, the Plane, Pine, Box, Blackthorn and Christmas Tree Fairies were fairies of the Trees, and the Rush-Grass, Cotton-Grass and Totter-Grass Fairies came from the Wayside. Now they are firmly established together as a collection that honours the plants and flowers that flourish in what Cicely Mary Barker called 'the grey of the year'.

Flower Fairies
of the Winter

The Snowdrop Fairy.

The Snowdrop Fairy

~ The Song of ~
The Snowdrop Fairy

Deep sleeps the Winter,
  Cold, wet, and grey;
Surely all the world is dead;
  Spring is far away.
Wait! the world shall waken;
  It is not dead, for lo,
The Fair Maids of February
  Stand in the snow!

~ THE SONG of ~ THE YEW FAIRY

Here, on the dark and solemn Yew,
   A marvel may be seen,
Where waxen berries, pink and new,
   Appear amid the green.

I sit a-dreaming in the tree,
   So old and yet so new;
One hundred years, or two, or three
   Are little to the Yew.

I think of bygone centuries,
   And seem to see anew
The archers face their enemies
   With bended bows of Yew.

The Yew Fairy

~ Snowdrop ~

Galanthus nivalis

There are few sights more welcome in the bleak days of winter than the delicate white bell of the Snowdrop. Said to resemble an angel on a snowflake, the dainty flowers give assurance that spring will come. Traditionally, the Snowdrop symbolises hope and purity. On the Feast of the Purification (2 February), it was a medieval custom for virgins, dressed in white, to bring posies of Snowdrops into church and strew them on the altar. This explains the Snowdrop's country name of 'fair maids of February', alluded to in the rhyme.

The Snowdrop is native to Britain and can still be seen growing wild in open woodland and hedgerows. It is a very popular garden plant and will spread to form patches beneath shrubs and trees, as well as naturalising easily in grass. Whether planted in drifts or in small groups to draw the eye, there is no doubting its impact on the winter garden. One of the most popular and reliable garden varieties is 'Flore Pleno', also known as the Double Snowdrop. It has many-petalled white flowers with green markings, and strong strap-shaped leaves. A taller Snowdrop variety is *Galanthus caucasicus*, which grows to about 25 centimetres, more than twice as high as its cousins. This striking Snowdrop has broad blue-green leaves and single pure-white flowers. All Snowdrops prefer moist soils.

Many gardeners find that Snowdrops can be difficult to grow from dry bulbs. It is possible to buy Snowdrops 'in the green', with leaves and flowers, and to plant them in the spring. They will usually establish themselves more easily.

~ *Yew* ~

Taxus baccata

The Yew played an important part in British history. As Cicely Mary Barker mentions in her rhyme, the long bows in the Middle Ages were made of Yew, which is very strong yet flexible. This gave the archers a much greater firing range than with bows made of lesser wood. Yew trees are long-lived but very slow growing, and in order to meet the demand for the wood, more Yews were planted. This caused some difficulty as all parts of the tree are poisonous to people and livestock and it should not be planted in fields or pasture. Some say this is the reason so many Yews were planted in churchyards.

The Yew's history goes back even further. The Druids held it sacred and used it in their religious rituals, planting it at their sacred sites. Yew trees continue to hold a fascination for us today. Some Yews in England are said to have been old when William the Conqueror landed. Perhaps because of its association with consecrated ground, it is believed to keep witches away. It symbolises sorrow.

The poison it contains, taxine, is now used in medicine.

The evergreen Yew is popular for garden hedging, though children must be warned that it is poisonous. Regular clipping eliminates the berries and encourages dense growth that is ideally suited to topiary. It will achieve a height of more than 20 metres if left unchecked. If growing Yew as a tree the variety 'Dovastonii Aurea' is an elegant choice. The golden foliage is held on tiers of horizontal branches. It is non-fruiting and will grow to approximately 5 metres.

The Winter Jasmine Fairy

~ The Song of ~
The Winter Jasmine Fairy

All through the Summer my leaves were green,
But never a flower of mine was seen;
Now Summer is gone, that was so gay,
And my little green leaves are shed away.
       In the grey of the year
       What cheer, what cheer?

The Winter is come, the cold winds blow;
I shall feel the frost and the drifting snow;
But the sun can shine in December too,
And this is the time of my gift to you.
       See here, see here,
       My flowers appear!

The swallows have flown beyond the sea,
But friendly Robin, he stays with me;
And little Tom-Tit, so busy and small,
Hops where the jasmine is thick on the wall;
       And we say: "Good cheer!
       We're here! We're here!"

～ The Song of ～
The Dead-Nettle Fairy

Through sun and rain, the country lane,
The field, the road, are my abode.
Though leaf and bud be splashed with mud,
Who cares? Not I!—I see the sky,
The kindly sun, the wayside fun
Of tramping folk who smoke and joke,
The bairns who heed my dusty weed
(No sting have I to make them cry),
And truth to tell, they love me well.
My brothers, White, and Yellow bright,
Are finer chaps than I, perhaps;
Who cares? Not I! So now good-bye.

The Dead-Nettle Fairy

The Rush-Grass and Cotton-Grass Fairies

~ The Song of ~
The Rush-Grass and
Cotton-Grass Fairies

Safe across the moorland
   Travellers may go,
If they heed our warning—
   We're the ones who know!

Let the footpath guide you—
   You'll be safely led;
There is bog beside you
   Where you cannot tread!

Mind where you are going!
   If you turn aside
Where you see us growing,
   Trouble will betide.

Keep you to the path, then!
   Hark to what we say!
Else, into the quagmire
   You will surely stray.

~ *Winter Jasmine* ~

Jasminum nudiflorum

This deciduous, winter-flowering shrub is not native to Britain but is now naturalised in many areas. It is a very rewarding plant, tolerant of all aspects and soil conditions, from a dry sunny site to deep shade, as long as its roots are not waterlogged. Deservedly popular, it flowers reliably year after year, its long slender shoots bearing cheerful yellow flowers through the winter and well into the spring.

~ *Dead-Nettle* ~

Lamium purpureum

The rather off-putting name of this plant refers to its close resemblance to the stinging nettle, but without the stinging hairs. It is very common in Britain and can be seen in fields, wasteland, roadsides and gardens.

The 'brothers, White, and Yellow bright' referred to in the rhyme are the White Dead-nettle *Lamium album* and the Yellow Archangel *Lamiastrum galeobdolon*.

~ Rush-Grass and Cotton-Grass ~

Juncus squarrosus and *Eriophorum angustifolium*

The Heath Rush is a native perennial, forming dense tufts easily recognized by the straight, tough flowering stem in the centre. It is common on acid soils on moorland heaths and bogs, especially where sheep grazing is heavy. It will grow up to half a metre in height.

The most attractive native rush grass is the Flowering Rush, *Butomus umbellatus*. This has been used in ornamental water gardens for centuries. Grown for its twisted, rush-like leaves and loose clusters of pale pink flowers, it is happiest when planted in full sun in any fertile soil in water up to 25 centimetres deep.

Rushes, with their strong but supple leaves have been used for weaving baskets from ancient times, and have thus earned the meaning of docility.

Cotton-grass is a member of the Sedge family of flowering grasses. The plants belonging to this family have characteristically triangular stems and are common in wet, marshy areas of Britain. They have an ecological importance because their root systems help to bind and stabilize soils. Cotton-grass is easily recognised by the creamy seedheads that look like tufts of cotton wool.

The stems and leaves of many of the Sedge grasses are used for weaving and papermaking. Most importantly, specific varieties of Cotton-grass grown in North America became the basis for the cotton industry that was a major part of the British Industrial Revolution.

The Spindle Berry Fairy

~ The Song of ~
The Spindle Berry Fairy

See the rosy-berried Spindle
All to sunset colours turning,
Till the thicket seems to kindle,
Just as though the trees were burning.
While my berries split and show
Orange-coloured seeds aglow,
One by one my leaves must fall:
Soon the wind will take them all.
Soon must fairies shut their eyes
For the Winter's hushabies;
But, before the Autumn goes,
Spindle turns to flame and rose!

~ THE SONG of ~
THE SHEPHERD'S PURSE FAIRY

Though I'm poor to human eyes
Really I am rich and wise.
Every tiny flower I shed
Leaves a heart-shaped purse instead.

In each purse is wealth indeed—
Every coin a living seed.
Sow the seed upon the earth—
Living plants shall spring to birth.

Silly people's purses hold
Lifeless silver, clinking gold;
But you cannot grow a pound
From a farthing in the ground.

Money may become a curse:
Give me then my Shepherd's Purse.

The
Shepherd's-Purse
Fairy.

The Shepherd's Purse Fairy

The Groundsel
Fairy.

The Groundsel Fairy

~ The Song of ~
The Groundsel Fairy

If dicky-birds should buy and sell
In tiny markets, I can tell
    The way they'd spend their money.
They'd ask the price of cherries sweet,
They'd choose the pinkest worms for meat,
And common Groundsel for a treat,
    Though *you* might think it funny.

Love me not, or love me well;
That's the way they'd buy and sell.

~ Spindle Berry ~

Euonymus europaeus

The Spindle Berry is common in hedgerows throughout Britain, especially on chalky or sandy soils. The flowers are generally inconspicuous, but as Cicely tells us in her rhyme, the leaves colour to a deep red in autumn, a show enhanced by the bright red or pink fruit. Most of the species are native to Europe. The wood from the Spindle Berry was once commonly used for carving. Later, as other more exotic woods replaced it, it was primarily used to make spindles – hence its name.

Many species of Euonymus are cultivated. The deciduous species such as *Euonymus alatus* are grown for their eye-catching autumn foliage and distinctive lobed fruit.

~ Shepherd's Purse ~

Capsella bursa-pastoris

As Cicely Mary Barker's rhyme suggests, this plant's attractive name comes from the purse-shaped seed-pod left after the flowers have fallen. Shepherd's Purse grows well on rich grassland and along embankments, and is common throughout Britain. It is a member of the

Mustard family and, like its cousins the Hedge Mustard and Winter-cress, prefers soil that is neither too wet nor too dry and is very rich in nutrients. Shepherd's Purse has a robust, earthy smell, which can be unpleasant after rain.

~ Groundsel ~

Senecio vulgaris

Groundsel is very common throughout Britain. It is found in gardens, fields and grasslands, particularly near ponds and ditches, as it prefers a damp site. After flowering the small white hairy fruits look a little like the white hair of an old man, and this is reflected in the Latin name *Senecio*, from *senex* – old man. As Cicely tells us in her rhyme, Groundsel is a popular treat for canaries and other birds.

Groundsel's most common garden relatives are asters, which bring welcome colour to the garden in late summer and autumn.

The autumn-flowering asters are known as Michaelmas daisies because they flower around Michaelmas (29 September), named after the church festival held in honour of St Michael, the archangel. These hardy perennials make a fine show in the border, particularly when planted in large single-coloured groups. Asters suffered a decline in popularity in recent years because of a perceived tendency to mildew. However, certain varieties have been bred to be mildew resistant. These include the *Aster x frikartii* cultivars and *Aster novae-angliae* 'Herbstschnee' (white) and 'Andenken an Alma Potschke' (cerise). The *Aster novae-angliae* cultivars require little staking.

The Lords-and-Ladies Fairy

~ The Song of ~
The Lords-and-Ladies Fairy

Fairies, when you lose your way,
From the dance returning,
In the darkest undergrowth
See my candles burning!
These shall make the pathway plain
Homeward to your beds again.

*(These are the berries of the Wild Arum, which has many
other names, and has a flower like a hood in the Spring.
The berries are not to be eaten.)*

~ The Song of ~
The Plane Tree Fairy

You will not find him in the wood,
    Nor in the country lane;
But in the city's parks and streets
    You'll see the Plane.

O turn your eyes from pavements grey,
    And look you up instead,
To where the Plane tree's pretty balls
    Hang overhead!

When he has shed his golden leaves,
    His balls will yet remain,
To deck the tree until the Spring
    Comes back again!

The Plane Tree Fairy

~ Lords-and-Ladies ~

Arum maculatum

Lords-and-Ladies are common in England and Wales, though rarer in Scotland because of their preference for warm situations. They enjoy loose, loamy soil, rich in nutrients, and are often found in woodland glades and along hedgerows. The flowers have an unmistakable hooded shape. Cicely Mary Barker drew Lords-and-Ladies in flower in *Flower Fairies of the Spring*. The colour of the pointed 'spadix' held within the hood can vary from white to violet, and it emits a rather unpleasant odour of decay in order to attract flies and other pollinating insects. In late summer the leaves and hood die back and are replaced with bright red berries.

All Arum berries are poisonous and the plant sap and berry juice can cause skin irritation.

~ Plane Tree ~

Platanus

'In the city's parks and streets \ You'll see the Plane.' As Cicely Mary Barker's rhyme suggests, Plane Trees are a familiar feature of our cities. They are tolerant of atmospheric pollution and are therefore widely planted in urban areas. The variety *Platanus x hispanica* is known as the London Plane because it is so common in that city. Plane Trees are less suitable for garden planting because of their enormous size (ultimately 45 metres) and the dense shade cast by their spreading branches. However, if given sufficient room, the distinctively mottled bark, strings of bristly fruits and glossy green leaves make the Plane Tree a handsome choice. Vigorous and uncomplicated, the Plane will grow in sun or shade in any soil.

The Plane Tree was popular in Ancient times. In Athens there was a long avenue of Plane Trees that became a meeting-place for Greek philosophers. Many hours were spent pacing up and down beneath the spreading branches whilst engaged in heated philosophical discussions. As a result, the Plane Tree was appointed the emblem of genius.

Folklore credits the Plane with medicinal virtues too. To heal general ills, simply chew the bark taken straight from the trunk. If taken for a cold, the bark should be boiled first.

The Burdock Fairy

~ THE SONG of ~
THE BURDOCK FAIRY

Wee little hooks on each brown little bur,
(Mind where you're going, O Madam and Sir!)
How they will cling to your skirt-hem and stocking!
Hear how the Burdock is laughing and mocking:
Try to get rid of me, try as you will,
Shake me and scold me, I'll stick to you still,
      I'll stick to you still!

~ The Song of ~
The Pine Tree Fairy

A tall, tall tree is the Pine tree,
    With its trunk of bright red-brown—
The red of the merry squirrels
    Who go scampering up and down.

There are cones on the tall, tall Pine tree,
    With its needles sharp and green;
Small seeds in the cones are hidden,
    And they ripen there unseen.

The elves play games with the squirrels
    At the top of the tall, tall tree,
Throwing cones for the squirrels to nibble—
    I wish I were there to see!

The Pine Tree Fairy

The Holly Fairy

～ THE SONG of ～
THE HOLLY FAIRY

O, I am green in Winter-time,
  When other trees are brown;
Of all the trees (So saith the rhyme)
  The holly bears the crown.
December days are drawing near
  When I shall come to town,
And carol-boys go singing clear
Of all the trees (O hush and hear!)
  The holly bears the crown!

For who so well-beloved and merry
As the scarlet Holly Berry?

~ *Burdock* ~

Arctium minus

Burdock is scattered throughout Britain. Most commonly found alongside paths and on wasteland, the plant will only grow where the soil is rich in nitrogen. Burdock flowers in mid to late summer, its purple thistle-like florets carried on erect branches. The leaves are large and slightly heart-shaped. The bracts are hooked and will cling to clothing or hair, enabling the plant to scatter its seeds over a wide area. This tenacity has made Burdock the symbol for importunity. The plant also carries the meaning 'touch me not', warning passers-by against becoming inextricably tangled with its burs. Burdock roots were once used to make a pain-relieving drink for women in labour.

~ *Pine Tree* ~

Pinus sylvestris

The Scots Pine is the only true British native pine. It is fast-growing when young but slows down with age, developing a flattened crown above a tall trunk which can be over 20 metres tall before the branches begin. The pine-cones are egg-shaped, ripening from green to brown and crack open in late summer to scatter the seeds. The cones themselves fall in large quantities in both autumn and spring. The Scots Pine will grow to more than 35 metres in height and is only suitable for the larger garden. However, some of its garden varieties have been bred to a smaller size.

~ Holly ~

Ilex aquifolium

The native Holly is common throughout Britain, found in deciduous and coniferous woods on all but very wet soils. It is very shade-tolerant, has shiny evergreen leaves and bears bright red berries from autumn through the depths of winter. Its blossom is usually white but insignificant. All holly berries are attractive to birds and sustain them when other foods are scarce. Surprisingly, Holly will grow up to 20 metres tall if left unchecked, making a conical tree.

Like the Yew, Holly was an important part of the Druids' religion. Its popularity has continued through the centuries, although its significance has changed. Decorating the house at Yuletide with branches of Holly and berries delighted the fairies and so brought good fortune. This tradition is still adhered to in many homes, though now it is considered part of the Christmas festival. The association between the Holly and the Ivy was a central part of the pagan religion. Holly, with its bright red berries, was seen as a symbol of the feminine aspect. Ivy was seen to represent the masculine. The ancient custom of decorating doorways with the plants intertwined was a symbolic union of the two.

The Box-Tree Fairy

~ The Song of ~ The Box-Tree Fairy

Have you seen the Box unclipped,
Never shaped and never snipped?
Often it's a garden hedge,
Just a narrow little edge;
Or in funny shapes it's cut,
And it's very pretty; *but*—

But, unclipped, it is a tree,
Growing as it likes to be;
And it has its blossoms too;
Tiny buds, the Winter through,
Wait to open in the Spring
In a scented yellow ring.

And among its leaves there play
Little blue-tits, brisk and gay.

~ THE SONG of ~
THE OLD-MAN'S BEARD FAIRY

This is where the little elves
Cuddle down to hide themselves;
Into fluffy beds they creep,
Say good-night, and go to sleep.

*(Old-Man's Beard is Wild Clematis; its flowers are called
Traveller's Joy. This silky fluff belongs to the seeds.)*

The Old-Man's Beard Fairy

~ Box Tree ~

Buxus sempervirens

The Box Tree is found throughout Britain but is particularly abundant in southern England. It is a slow-growing evergreen shrub that prefers chalk or limestone soils and can be found in sunny, open locations as well as shady beech woods. If left unchecked as Cicely Mary Barker's rhyme suggests, it can achieve the height of a small tree. It flowers in mid to late spring, carrying small yellow blossoms in clusters where the leaf joins the stem.

Unaffected by the changing of the seasons, its enduring qualities have made Box ideal for use in topiary, and it has become the symbol of stoicism.

Dwarf hedges used in parterres are traditionally composed of Box. The deep green glossy foliage contrasts well with bright flowers and gravel paths. The smaller cultivars can be easily grown in pots and are useful for a formal design. The garden varieties include 'Elegantissima', a compact bush with variegated cream and green leaves, and 'Suffruticosa', a small shrub traditonally used for edging flowerbeds. The leaves are very dense and can be clipped hard every year.

~ Old-Man's Beard Fairy ~

Clematis vitalba

The feathery white seedheads of Old-Man's Beard scrambling through hedgerows and thickets are a common sight in winter. They are the fruits of the native wild clematis, which is found throughout southern England and Wales. It is seldom seen further north than South Yorkshire because of its preference for warmth and it has colonised only moderately hilly areas.

The clematis has a woody climbing stem with heart-shaped leaves. Its flowers are made up of creamy, petal-like sepals, and its sweet fragrance makes its other common name, Traveller's Joy, very well deserved. Cicely Mary Barker included Traveller's Joy in *Flower Fairies of the Summer*.

The juice of the wild clematis can sting the skin and beggars used it to cause ugly sores on their skin and so evoke greater pity from passers-by. This led to it becoming the emblem of artifice and deception.

There are several different types of clematis that flower happily in the garden. Probably the best-known varieties are the large-flowered hybrids, which bloom mainly in the summer. These are available in many colours and will scramble happily over shrubs or up walls and fences. They seldom grow more than 3 metres high.

The Blackthorn Fairy

~ The Song of ~
The Blackthorn Fairy

The wind is cold, the Spring seems long
 a-waking;
   The woods are brown and bare;
Yet this is March: soon April will be making
   All things most sweet and fair.

See, even now, in hedge and thicket tangled,
   One brave and cheering sight:
The leafless branches of the Blackthorn,
   spangled
   With starry blossoms white!

*(The cold days of March are sometimes called
Blackthorn Winter".)*

~ The Song of ~
The Hazel-Catkin Fairy

Like little tails of little lambs,
    On leafless twigs my catkins swing;
They dingle-dangle merrily
    Before the wakening of Spring.

Beside the pollen-laden tails
    My tiny crimson tufts you see
The promise of the autumn nuts
    Upon the slender hazel tree.

While yet the woods lie grey and still
    I give my tidings: "Spring is near!"
One day the land shall leap to life
    With fairies calling: "Spring is HERE!"

The
Hazel-Catkin
Fairy.

The Hazel-Catkin Fairy

~ *Blackthorn* ~

Prunus spinosa

The black bark and thorny twigs of this hardy native shrub make it easily identifiable. The white blossom appears before the leaves, and the twigs and flowers make a striking contrast. Blackthorn is common in hedgerows and along verges throughout Britain. In the autumn it bears blue-black, sour sloe berries, which give it its other common name, Sloe.

The berries can be used to make the very potent 'Sloe gin'. Cicely drew the Sloe Fairy in *Flower Fairies of the Autumn*.

The blossom first appears in March, often coinciding with a sharp spell of frost. As Cicely tells us, country people call this time 'Blackthorn winter'. Blackthorn's sharp spines are notoriously difficult to untangle from the clothes on which they cling and it has therefore become the emblem for difficulty. However, its persistent flowering through the cold days has also given it a happier significance; that of constancy.

Blackthorn has many garden relatives, all of which bear wonderful spring blossom.

~ Hazel-Catkin ~

Corylus avellana

The Hazel tree, with its pretty yellow catkins in spring and hazelnuts in the autumn is a striking small tree found throughout Britain. According to ancient lore, the little hazelnut embodied knowledge, wisdom and fertility. One Celtic legend tells how a Hazel tree dropped its nuts into a well below it. A salmon swimming in the well ate the hazelnuts. Fionn, a Celtic hero, caught the salmon and cooked it. While he was eating the salmon Fionn tasted one of the nuts it had swallowed and instantly gained all knowledge. For this reason, the hazelnut symbolized wisdom. Cicely has a Hazel-Nut Fairy in *Flower Fairies of the Autumn*.

The Hazel is said to be a lucky tree. A cap of Hazel leaves and twigs ensures safety at sea, while a sprig of Hazel will protect from lightning. Water diviners use Hazel wands to search for hidden springs. For more general use the Hazel's flexibility makes it ideal as an alternative to willow and wicker in baskets and garden decorations.

The Totter-Grass Fairy

66

～ The Song of ～
The Totter-Grass Fairy

The leaves on the tree-tops
    Dance in the breeze;
Totter-grass dances
    And sways like the trees—

Shaking and quaking!
    While through it there goes,
Dancing, a Fairy,
    On lightest of toes.

(Totter-grass is also called Quaking-grass.)

~ The Song of ~
The Winter Aconite Fairy

Deep in the earth
I woke, I stirred.
I said: "Was that the Spring I heard?
For something called!"
"No, no," they said;
"Go back to sleep. Go back to bed.

"You're far too soon;
The world's too cold
For you, so small." So I was told.
But how could I
Go back to sleep?
I could not wait; I had to peep!

Up, up, I climbed,
And here am I.
How wide the earth! How great the sky!
O wintry world,
See me, awake!
Spring calls, and comes; 'tis no mistake.

The Winter Aconite Fairy

～ Totter-Grass ～

Briza media

This native perennial is found throughout the British Isles on most types of grassland, though most common on the chalky ground of southern England. It is tolerant of heavy and poorly drained soils. Totter-grass has little value for grazing as it produces very few leaves. However, the dangling heart-shaped flower heads shaking in the breeze make it one of the most attractive grasses, and it is often dried and used for winter flower arrangements. The variety 'Limouzi' has larger flower-heads and grey-green leaves.

Cicely also includes Totter-grass's other name, Quaking-grass.

Grasses are an often under-used feature in the garden. For many people, grass means the lawn. However, many grasses make effective specimen plants and look attractive in borders, their feathery foliage and flowers bringing movement into the garden as they sway in the breeze. A great bonus is that grasses need little attention and yet have a long season of interest. What they lack in colour they more than make up for with their sculptural leaves and flowerheads.

The true grass family, the *Gramineae*, includes the bamboo and pampas grasses. Bamboos are an essential element in a Japanese style garden. They make good screens and their dramatic combination of tall canes and rustling evergreen foliage also makes them a splendid focal point. The flowerheads, produced in mid summer, are a dull brown and can make the bamboo look untidy. However, as plants bloom at irregular intervals, some only every hundred years, this is not a significant problem. Bamboos are generally hardy but prefer a sunny position. When choosing a bamboo variety it is best to check whether they are clump-forming or have running rhizomes which need to be confined lest they take over the garden.

Pampas grass (*Cortaderia selloana*) forms dense clumps of arching, evergreen leaves and tall stems bearing showy silvery plumes up to 45 centimetres long. These are produced in late summer and last into winter.

~ Winter Aconite ~

Eranthis hyemalis

The Winter Aconite is one of the first flowers to bloom in spring, sometimes even before the snowdrop. The cheerful yellow flowers peep out from their ruffs of feathery green leaves and look a little like oversized buttercups. Winter Aconites like well-drained soil and some shade in the summer, so the protection of deciduous shrubs or trees is ideal. The plants grow to about 10 centimetres in height and multiply rapidly, eventually forming a charming floral carpet.

Winter Aconites look at their best when planted in large groups, perhaps naturalized in a shrub border or beneath trees. They associate particularly well with the blue or white stars of *Anemone blanda*. Like snowdrops, Winter Aconites can be a little difficult to establish when planted as dry tubers. Many nurseries sell them 'in the green' to be planted in early spring. When the foliage has faded it can be raked off.

The Christmas Tree Fairy

~ THE SONG of ~
THE CHRISTMAS TREE FAIRY

The little Christmas Tree was born
    And dwelt in open air;
It did not guess how bright a dress
    Some day its boughs would wear;
Brown cones were all, it thought, a tall
    And grown-up Fir would bear.

O little Fir! Your forest home
    Is far and far away;
And here indoors these boughs of yours
    With coloured balls are gay,
With candle-light, and tinsel bright,
    For this is Christmas Day!

A dolly-fairy stands on top,
    Till children sleep; then she
(A live one now!) from bough to bough
    Goes gliding silently.
O magic sight, this joyous night!
    O laden, sparkling tree!

~ Christmas Tree ~

Pinaceae

It is difficult to imagine Christmas without a Christmas tree. The dark green needles of a fir tree decorated with twinkling candles are a common sight, not only in houses but also in shop windows, market squares and even above the heads of the hurrying shoppers. The Christmas Tree is a central part of the Christmas tradition. It is therefore remarkable that the first Christmas tree came to Britain as recently as 1834, when Prince Albert brought a fir tree to Windsor Castle from his native Germany as a present for Queen Victoria. As with most traditions, however, the roots of the decorated festive tree go back for thousands of years. Many cultures saw the evergreens, which remain green even in winter, as a symbol of life even during the dead season. To decorate with evergreen trees and branches was a way of celebrating eternal life.

The Romans celebrated Saturnalia, their winter festival, by decorating evergreen trees with small, shining pieces of metal in honour of Saturn, the god of metalwork and agriculture. In the Middle Ages, a fir tree was decorated with apples and given the name Paradise Tree as part of the feast of Adam and Eve, held on 24 December.

It was Martin Luther, the great German protestant reformer who is believed to have been the first to decorate an indoor Christmas tree. After a midnight walk through a peaceful pine forest, with the bright stars shining above his head, he tried to recreate the experience for his family by bringing a tree into the house and decorating it with candles. The decorated tree grew in popularity in Germany and Austria, and German settlers in eastern Pennsylvania brought the custom to the United States. Since then the tradition has become established throughout the Western world.

Although we speak of a Christmas Tree, there are many different species that are grown for the purpose. The best-selling trees are the Scotch pine, Douglas fir, Noble fir and Norway Spruce. The Norway Spruce was traditionally the species used to decorate British homes. It was native to the British Isles before the last Ice Age and was reintroduced before the 1500s. Nowadays, however, the different species are grown commercially and it is even possible to choose and fell your own.

The fairy on the top of the Christmas Tree is a very British tradition. In the rest of Europe and Scandinavia a star or angel is the preferred ornament. Quite why the fairy is so popular in this country is unknown, but perhaps it reflects the depth of the Faerie tradition which was driven underground by the arrival of Christianity but continued to be observed at sacred sites such as local wells, springs and trees. Nowadays fairies are thought of as harmless and friendly beings, but for centuries fairies were believed to be tricky, fickle, even malevolent, and they had to be placated with offerings. Country people gave them the name 'Little Folk', in the hope that the pleasant name would rub off on the fairies. The ancient Greeks did the same when they called the terrible Furies 'the Kindly Ones'. It is therefore possible that the Christmas Tree fairy is a remnant of a far older, pagan tradition, perhaps associated with the Winter Solstice, or Yule.

THE TRADTIONAL
~ MEANINGS and USES of PLANTS ~

The relationship between the mediaeval peasant and his garden was intensely practical. The small plot of earth surrounding the peasant's house was stocked with basic beans and herbs that could be used for cooking. At that time the only people who had the leisure time available to create anything remotely decorative were the nobility and the monasteries, and even they were more likely to favour a plant with medicinal virtues or a pleasant scent and taste.

It was Henry VIII's dissolution of the Monasteries that led to the first great change in the peasant's garden. Villagers were now cut off from the herbal medicines that had once been supplied by the monks, and so they began to grow their own; most taken from the old monastery gardens. The traditional names have great charm. Comfrey's other names include 'knitbone' and 'boneset', referring to the belief that it would help to knit broken bones. Golden rod's chief use was for staunching blood from wounds. In some cases, science has proved the monks and the peasants right. Garlic was valued as an antiseptic even in ancient times. More recently the antiseptic properties of garlic have been scientifically proven. An even better example is the opium poppy, which has been known as a drug for relieving the pains of cholera and childbirth for at least two thousand years. Today the chief ingredient of some headache pills, codeine, is produced from the poppy's milky juice. The better known medicine taken from the poppy is morphine.

Less scientific, but charming nevertheless, is the ancient Doctrine of Signatures. It was believed that when the devil let loose disease and pestilence on the earth, God gave us the antidotes in plants throughout our countryside; and that each plant was stamped with a characteristic, or Signature, that tells us how to use it. Probably the best known example is lungwort, whose foliage has white spots. These were thought to resemble the lung scars caused by tuberculosis, and the plant was much sought after as a cure. Science has been unable to substantiate that particular belief, but lungwort is still recommended by some herbalists to treat coughs.

Other plants liberated from the monasteries were grown to add savour to the basic vegetables and meat, often rancid, that was the peasants' diet. Borage added flavour to soup and could be used to make a refreshing tonic. In addition, its young leaves and flowers were added to salads. Dill was used to flavour stews and vinegar, as well as making the ideal fish sauce. Fennel was another favourite, particularly for cheese, fish and pickles, while sage became the ideal accompaniment for pork, chicken and veal. Mint was widely used in drinks and as a sauce for meat, and it was also an important ingredient in many of the alcoholic drinks made by the monks (medicinal, of course!). Other herbs helped to mask the dreadful smells that built up in the small, crowded, rush-strewn houses. A few branches of rosemary or lavender might be scattered through the rooms and perhaps sandwiched between stored clothing in trunks or chests. There were also plants used for making dyes, such as golden rod for yellow and irises for black. There were still more plants that were grown purely for their help in warding off evil. When life was so precarious, it is no wonder that people clung to the hope that certain plants might offer protection. Yew, elder and bay trees were planted partly in order to protect the house from witches. Columbine was believed to protect from plague, as was the wood anemone.

To the medieval peasant the plants were useful in all these different ways, yet their beauty was in many ways incidental, a bonus. Gradually, however, as more gardens were planted with herbs and shrubs, neighbours would barter for cuttings, or plants might be given as gifts. Often the housewife would take over the little plot and might interplant the herbs and vegetables with wild plants seen in the hedgerow; primroses, bluebells, violets and foxgloves. As the centuries passed, more plants became available. Workers at the 'big house' might bring back cuttings of roses and peonies. In the late eighteenth century, when the gentry were creating ornamental parks under the influence of Capability Brown, the estate workers brought home many of the plants that had been discarded by their masters. Thus the true cottage garden was born, with all the plants mingled in a glorious riot of colour that has become the hallmark of the traditional English garden.